The Sword of Io

a Night Stalkers 2352 short story

by

M. L. Buchman

Buchman Bookworks

Other works by M.L. Buchman

The Night Stalkers
The Night Is Mine
I Own the Dawn
Daniel's Christmas
Wait Until Dark
Frank's Independence Day
Peter's Christmas
Take Over at Midnight
Light Up the Night

Firehawks
Pure Heat
Wildfire at Dawn
Full Blaze

Angelo's Hearth
Where Dreams are Born
Where Dreams Reside
Maria's Christmas Table
Where Dreams Unfold
Where Dreams Are Written

Dieties Anonymous
Cookbook from Hell: Reheated
Saviors 101

Thrillers
Swap Out!
One Chef

SF/F Titles
Nara

Monk's Maze

1

"*Well, that sucked.*"

Christine lay on her suit's backpack and stared up at Jupiter through her visor. No visible cracks, and she was still breathing O2-mix, that was a good start. Her suit wasn't overheating or freezing, that was better. She turned her head to look around for who had spoken, but her neck hurt from the crash so she stopped moving. All she could see was sky, unless she sat up.

Christine wasn't ready to risk trying that just yet.

"That really sucked." Parello. Her new side gunner. She recognized his voice this time. Less than a week in the squad, he'd transferred in from D company. Knew it was him because it was the only voice she didn't know like her own heartbeat. Also, he sounded like he actually came from Earth rather than one of the inner colonies. Nobody came from Earth anymore.

"Anyone else?" There should be twenty answers, there was only the one.

"Hey, Captain Christine the Fighting Machine! You made it, sir!"

"Don't call me that, Sergeant."

"Why not? Your reputation reaches far and wide. Guess you earned it, too. There is no way in hell we should be alive."

"Let's check suit integrity then see if we're the only ones." But she lay there a moment longer looking up at the gas giant. Her back was on Io, and the planet named for the god of thunder filled a quarter of the sky, forty degrees of arc.

Jupiter felt as if it filled her whole world and was crushing down upon her chest. She could see every band, every swirl and detail as if she hovered just over the cloudy surface rather than lying on her back like some stunned-puppy recruit four-hundred thousand klicks away.

Everything was so vibrant, right down to her own stink in the suit's air recyclers. She'd never come so close to death before, maybe that's what did it, made everything seem so alive. Even if they were on a dead moon.

Shock. She was in shock from the crash and had to get moving. Her first attempt to sit up almost elicited a groan from all of the muscles she'd wrenched.

"I'd be glad to check on my suit's systems, sir, but I can't see shit."

Christine nudged the heads-up display with her chin. Toggled to the third screen. The Health and Usage Monitoring System reported that she had a full load: O2, water, ammo. Screen four of the HUMS reported that her O2 scrubber, tracking, command,

and waste recycling were okay. Though she wasn't impressed with the hundred percent suit integrity rating. After what they'd just been through that couldn't be accurate; but at least she wasn't leaking.

Then she hit the squad screen.

Two signals. Her and Parello. Emma and Marko were gone. She hit the extended menu which should have give her the read on the troops from the Royal Marines they'd been trying to deliver to the backside of Europa.

Flatlines.

She forced herself upright and scanned the Ionian hillside in the shadowless half-light of Jupiter. Scattered bodies. Not even someone with just a dead radio. No movement, except herself and Parello. He sat upright with his back toward her.

"Just the two of us."

"Maybe the circuit's just gone bad."

She could see the entire half platoon of Her Majesty's Special Operations Forces scattered across the broad hillside of yellow volcanic ash. Knowing they were going down hard, she'd ejected the troops at twenty meters up, giving her shot-up Stinger ship all the braking thrust she'd dared right before kicking them loose. Damned spaceship's HUMS hadn't tracked something that was damaged, they were always slow to update on mechanical faults in a catastrophe. She should have allowed for that, but there hadn't been time. Not with how imminent their crash had been.

Whatever it was, it had been too much and the Stinger had shredded right in the middle of the squad, each soldier falling slowly in the light gravity. Half had already been dead from the attack, the other half… She didn't see a whole lot of hope that anyone else was alive.

She headed over in Parello's direction, just two careful long strides in the fifteen percent Earth-normal grav. Christine dug in a heel to stop and cursed when she turned and saw Parello's face plate, his entire visor was one big star crack. There was no way it should still be intact.

"You okay in there, Sergeant?"

"Trying not to breath hard. Puff of air hits this wrong and it's really going to ruin my day."

Christine hated shit like this. They all practiced something like a helmet change in atmo a thousand times so that it was instinct, but you were never dumb enough to try it in the field. Not until you had to. She didn't know anyone who'd had to. At least not that lived to tell about it.

She didn't need to check the readout on the body lying not far from Parello; a spar of the Stinger's landing strut was punched through the suit's chest. With a quick slap, she released the latch and twisted the helmet free, barely registering the thick red hair that had made Andrews so easy to spot in a crowd. No blood inside the helmet.

"Ready to change helmets in five," she told Parello.

He reached up to unfasten his own latch. His hands appeared steady.

Good man.

Per training, she spoke calm and steady by rote. "Final deep breath. Close eyes. Remember to exhale slowly. And. Now!"

Parello spun the helmet off, the visor shattering even as he did so, tiny shards blowing outward to ping lightly against her own visor. He quickly dumped his helmet straight back, again per training, getting both it and his arms out of her way. She slapped Corporal Andrews' helmet on him and gave it a twist to seat the latch. "Continue to exhale for five." She knew her voice would sound thin as the helmet pressurized.

After five seconds, Parello opened his eyes, then blinked a couple times.

"You've got pretty eyes, Captain Merrill. How come I never noticed that before?"

"Because you just transferred in last week. Still glad you did?" She was going to ignore the "pretty eyes" remark. They allowed cross-rank relationships now, had for a century, but she'd always found it useful to keep her distance when in command. Actually, to keep her distance from anyone.

"I'm alive. So, it's working for me." He started tapping his chin to toggle the display. "Oh crap! Literally."

"What?"

"My crapper's gone. No wonder my ass hurts." He shifted his hips back and forth on the ground and grimaced.

She flipped him over, on Io he weighed about as much as a sack of potatoes. Sure enough, his suit's recycling unit had taken a direct hit. Probably all that saved his life as something had hit it real damn hard. That shock would have gone right up the pickup funnel pushed partway inside him. Must have hurt like a son of a bitch.

"Detach that one for me, will you?" Christine pointed to the recycling unit on the closest body lying just a half-dozen paces off. Staff Sergeant Halberson's suit. Knew it was him by the sheer size of the man, didn't even know suits came that big before she met him. Got to be a weird kinda jock to sign up for a career in cramped space quarters when you were that size. Of course, the Special Operations Royal Marines were nuts to begin with anyway.

Then she looked away, trying not to think of the man it had kept alive for months at a time, until ten minutes ago when all his air had rushed out into this moon's vacuum through his crushed helmet.

Compartmentalize.

Time to think later about how much she'd miss his quiet anchoring of the Special Ops team.

"How did a woman with such pretty eyes go officer?" Parello set to work on Halberson's suit.

It wasn't a story she typically told. Okay, not one she ever told. To anyone. But she also had never been one of two survivors on a small airless bluff orbiting Jupiter surrounded by the dead and the thousand fragments of a shattered Stinger.

Parello was off to a good start, fishing wrenches and sealant out of Halberson's emergency pouch rather than using any of his own fresh supplies. She knew it still felt you were robbing the dead, but Parello clearly had soldiered long enough to understand the necessity of keeping his own supplies fully stocked for as long as possible. He was steady enough to be strategizing his own survival.

She shrugged to herself, her past would give them something to distract themselves with. They probably wouldn't make it anyway.

Parello loosened the first hoses on Halberson's recycler.

"It was my dad," she kept her words short because her jaw was clamped so tight.

"In the service? He proud when you made Captain?"

How did Parello keep his voice so steady? Christine also resisted the urge to open her own kit rather than plunder the dead. She moved over to Lieutenant Perkins' suit and almost succeeded in ignoring the missing legs. It was only the Lieutenant's third offensive and now she'd never have a chance to fulfill her academy potential.

She'd been a good pilot, but not great. Hadn't stopped Christine from liking her, but neither did it stop her wondering if they'd all still be alive if Emma had been better.

Probably not, the attacker had come out of nowhere. They'd managed to kill it, but not before the damage was done.

Christine pulled the tool pouch off what remained of Perkin's thigh, making it wave its blackened-blood stump obscenely at her. Then she moved across the detritus of Io's volcanic madness and knelt down behind Parello, the yellow sulfur ash crunching beneath her heavily padded knees.

"Never told him I was in the service. Never had the chance."

"Oh, sorry, didn't know he was dead."

Christine focused on placing all of the tools on the ash, in the order she'd need them.

Parello finished freeing the recycle unit from the base of Halberson's pack and passed it back to her. Then he dropped down on all fours with his backside to her. A number of inappropriate jokes came to mind, none of which would be funny at the moment.

"I joined to undo some of what he did," Christine made sure the replacement unit was oriented in the right direction. With the wrench, she pre-loosened the hose lock-rings on either end of Parello's shattered unit, then undid the four retaining clips.

"Old man was a real cut up?"

"Why do you say that, Sergeant?"

"Because, Captain Christine the Fighting Machine, you are one squared away, hard-ass. And I mean that in the best of ways, sir."

"Shut up, Parello."

"Yes, sir, Captain Merrill, sir."

Christine inspected everything again, making sure it was all set. Then prelit the torch. No need to conserve supplies, more were scattered far and wide around them.

"Do it already!" Parello's voice wasn't so easy.

She could hear the strain starting to take hold beneath his easy surface. It made her like him more. He'd just proven he was capable of being an optimist in a scary situation, but not a gung-ho space jock.

His record showed problems with authority, but a kick-ass battle record with an amazing ability to survive. One of the reasons she'd accepted him into E Company 5th battalion of the fighting 160th.

She took her time making sure everything was ready. The surface of Io allowed no room for mistakes.

"Death Waits in the Dark" had been the Night Stalkers' motto on Earth when they flew helicopters on night operations. After the move to space, it was only natural that the 160th would remain at the flight controls. When the U.S. had ceased to exist in any form but the Night Stalkers hadn't, they were folded into the remains of King Richards British empire out in the Colony Cans whirling around at the LaGrange 2 point behind the Moon.

"Okay," she said it as matter-of-factly as she could, partly for her own nerves to steady her hands, but partly to keep Parello calm now that she'd heard the edge. "Okay, this is gonna feel a little weird."

"No shit!" Then he barked out a laugh on the unintended pun that neither of them commented on. They both knew this was far less likely to work than a helmet change.

"Merrill is my mom's name. My dad is General Ansel Moore."

As Parello was distracted by her statement, not even managing a low whistle of surprise, Christine snapped open the two fittings she'd already loosened. Pulling hard on the recycling unit, Parello grunted.

"Ansel Moore," he managed it through gritted teeth.

"Yep!" She twisted and pulled to break the sealant and the unit came free from his suit, including the collecting funnel. She tossed it aside.

Flash the torch briefly on Halberson's unit to get the funnel up to somewhere around body temperature, maybe even sterilize it a bit. Careful not to melt it.

Smear sealant around the edges.

Line it up. And...

She slammed her palm into the unit to seat it firmly.

Inserted.

"Shit that's cold! General...'The Sword' Moore...is your...old man." He grunted out each phrase as she used the clamps and mounting screws to shove the unit home. "But he started the damn war!"

Her father still wore an old-style U.S. Marine Corps Mameluke officer's sword, which was considered a bit of a slap in the face to the British generals who wore a similar blade. He'd been known to dispense justice, at least his form of it, with the brutal blade and earned his nickname.

It took Christine another thirty seconds to finish the field repair and run a second line of seal around the edges just in case. It was ugly, nowhere near by-the-book, but it would keep Parello alive.

"So," he was taking deep breaths that echoed loudly over the suit radio as he struggled to retain control. "That's…why you said you…were making up for him."

"Check function." Now she wanted him to back off that topic. Was sorry she'd even brought it up to begin with. She heard him clicking through the menus.

"HUMS shows good. Damn I'm glad that's over. Nothing like showing off your backside to a beautiful officer."

"You mean your best side?" A tease? Surprised herself; she never teased.

"Not the most attractive view? Damn and I had such hopes, Captain Merrill." He turned gingerly until he was facing her, kind of working his hips to seat the unit more comfortably, if there was such a thing. One of the many things a space grunt learned to live with. Just not often with someone else's shit mixed in with their own.

She couldn't look away from his dark eyes when they were finally turned visor to visor.

"Having him for an old man is too much for anyone to make up for." He sounded far more wise and insightful about her than she ever wanted anyone to be.

"I was always an overachiever." Truth. So done with the subject, she nodded downward as much as you could in a suit.

"And that's a cute ass." Also truth, and not the best choice of new topic for keeping her distance. But she'd been in the suit locker when everyone was stripping down and gearing up. Even among the fine physical conditioning of all her troops, Parello had stood out as an exceptional example. Not a thing wrong with his body.

2

Christine had a lot of time to consider that remark about his cute ass over the next two days.

They made quick work of checking all the other bodies, loading up on all the gear they could. Focusing on water, air, and ammo; the three essentials. Only then did they plug every empty space in their packs with non-essentials like food packs.

Parello managed to cobble together enough gear to get a radio squirt out to command.

The message back said pickup in two days.

Christine made a quick sketch in the sand. "We're here, a hundred klicks east of Ionian Mons. Just north of the equator and thirty degrees off the center line with Jupiter. So…" She did her best to remember her geography, because the onboard systems were scattered across a half kilometer of wreckage. "Tell them we'll meet them at the neck of the Shakuru Patera."

"Damn, Captain. Isn't that like a thousand kilometers? Why are we doing that?"

"Tell them, Sergeant."

He told them, then they loaded up and got underway. They set off at an easy lope, the gravity only a little higher than the Earth's Moon. Parello took the first turn at point, though he left his recoilless SCAR rifle Velcroed against his suit's chest plate. Her own Space Combat Assault Rifle thumped against her chest with the familiarity of her own beating heart.

"Look up," she told him. He'd left his concern about the distance open, but hadn't questioned her orders. Even in this day and age there were still men who didn't trust women in the Army, but apparently he wasn't one of them.

Parello looked up. Not an easy maneuver in a suit while trotting along under light gravity and a double load of supplies. But he did it. Here was a soldier who understood his own body and had clearly trained it into a finely honed tool.

"Jupiter." He still didn't get it.

"We're thirty degrees off the primary flux corridor between Jupiter and Io. Radiation levels are a hundred times Earth Orbit. That's how Moore's ship hid from us, they rode right up the center of the corridor." Io, like Earth's Moon, spun only once per orbit, always keeping the same face toward the lethal Jupiter.

"Damn. No way they were shielded for that. Doesn't the man even care about his own troops?"

"He doesn't even care about his own daughter." The bile was bitter in her throat as she fought back against the anger. Damn, it hurt worse every time she thought about it, not less.

"All he cared about was his goddamn crusade against the royals of the colonies. It killed Mom. He just broke her heart and it killed her."

"A thousand klicks," Parello rolled the idea around on his tongue, decent enough to spare her the inquisition of the chunk of her soul she'd just heaved up on the Ionian surface.

She couldn't speak yet, but she could kiss the man for his decency of ignoring her outburst.

"That gets us almost ninety degrees to the northwest of the corridor. Our suits aren't rated for two days at the radiation levels at that crash site. And we couldn't cobble together a shelter at the Stinger, in case the bad guys come looking."

"Dead on." Nothing wrong with Parello's brain either.

"At fifteen percent gravity, that's like a hundred and fifty kilometer hike in two days with a double-load pack."

Christine waited for it. Nothing a grunt hated worse than long hikes. They did it. But a pair of seventy-five klick hikes back to back over unknown terrain was brutal no matter how you cut it.

"Guess the rumors were true, Captain."

"Which ones?"

"The ones about you being a hard-ass, sir. I like that in a commander. Fits me down to my toes." He settled into that steady ground-eating lope that a trained soldier learned, or fell by the wayside. He adjusted his rhythm to Io's gravity about as fast as she did, and she was left to follow along and contemplate his cute ass.

3

They switched off the lead every hour after a five-minute break. Their long march slowly shifted Jupiter, from its fixed position almost directly over the crash site, down toward the horizon behind them. They followed slowly lengthening shadows—for Jupiter was far brighter than the sun on Io's surface—as they trudged northwest from the crash site. The farther they walked, the deeper and darker the shadows became on the far side of anything that rose above the plain.

Helmet lights were often needed, despite the drain on batteries, to make sure there were no pits or jagged edges lurking within the pitch dark of a hill's shade.

It was relaxing to be able to simply follow and let someone else scout the best path through the nightmare landscape for an hour at a time.

Volcanic peaks towered above them, over a thousand volcanoes shredded the moon's surface, and a lot of them were active. They had to cut north to avoid a plume spewing sulfur oxides into the sky. About half of the ejecta fell back to the surface, but the other half achieved escape velocity and added to the sulfur belt that Io was leaving in its path.

Their suits slowly yellowed with the accumulation of dust.

Parello made jokes about never having wanted to kiss Halberson, let alone share his recycler.

Christine answered his questions about her service. He asked about her mother too, but was smart enough not to ask about the rebellion's leader.

General "The Sword" Moore had been respectable once, a top commander who'd made his name back in the Colony Wars. Then, after peace had finally been built over five long years, he turned terrorist. There was no other word for it. His rhetoric against the Richards Monarchy had been vitriolic. When Richards was voted in by all of the remaining colonies, the decision had stuck in his craw.

"Only the military finished the Colony Wars. Only the military understands how to keep the solar system running."

His rebellion had been put down, and put down hard. He'd escaped out past the asteroid belt with a small cadre of hard-liners and too much equipment. The "Hero of the War" had become the "Terrorist of the Monarchy."

Special Operations Forces had been sent out after him and the Night Stalkers flew them there.

They were squeezing "The Sword" hard; they'd driven him out of the asteroid belt rock by bloody rock and flanked him to take back Saturn. The Jovian system was the last of his strongholds. But he wasn't done yet. With sixty-seven moons and four rings, the terrorists had dug in deep. And Europa, with its water oceans comprising the best reaction mass in the outer system, was so heavily fortified that it was impregnable—at least so far.

Parello had apparently been born the day he joined the Army. It took her until late in the second day of the hike, when they were both moving far too slowly, before she figured it out. Her thoughts had been on the blisters that she couldn't treat, couldn't even massage inside her boots.

So, she'd forced her thoughts to something more pleasant. Last night she and Parello had sat side by side on the ash surface, a tri-layer aluminized sheet laid over them for radiation protection, blocking any view of the stars or Jupiter.

It had been cozy.

Neither of them much interested in sleep, they'd actually shifted until they were shoulder to shoulder. Even through the heavy suits it had been nice to feel another human being. They leaned against a rock outcropping, because there was no real way to lie down comfortably in a full field suit, even at fifteen percent gravity.

They'd talked of relationships and friends. Parello clearly had his fair share of both.

"Looking the way you do, how can you not have had more men than that?" Parello had been shocked.

"Officer. Hello. Don't fraternize with the troops or it makes it harder to give and take orders, even if it is accepted now. And being…" she couldn't say it directly. "…the daughter of who I am, I found it easier to keep to myself."

Parello was easy to talk to. It was as comfortable as she'd been with anyone since her mother's death. More than once they'd clunked their helmets together so that she could hear his deep laugh through conduction rather than the radio. They'd finally slept tipped together.

Christine considered asking Parello about his real past. He'd been subtle about it, yet candid about everything since joining the Army. Criminal? Didn't get you into Special Operations. Not that a record kept you out, but it took a kind of determination and grit to make the grade that didn't come easy. Enjoying hard work wasn't why a man typically turned criminal.

But she couldn't ask.

They were in "The Grind" now, far past talking. They'd covered over a thousand kilometers. It was a landscape from hell. Jupiter irradiating them from behind, they each had a silver foil blanket draped over their packs as extra protection. Before them lay the yellow-gray sulfurous plains. They had to climb old lava flows while avoiding two hotspots more heated than the face of Mercury. They'd been forced north by the active Girru Patera, then forced south by the

Heiseb Patera flow. The sun appeared as a blinding spot the size of a fingertip held at arm's length. It made travel easier for a while as it lit the shadows, but was soon gone as Io followed his day-and-a-half orbit around Jupiter.

In the heart of the grind, a soldier just folds into herself. A space where the body was past agony and it was now a contest of wills.

No way on this moon was Christine going to be beat by a lousy walk. She'd survived nearly a decade of service, and her father's shock troops were not going to end her. If she had to take the battle to him personally, so be it. No way were they getting past her.

Still, it was easier due to Parello's silent company. His early complaining had all been perfunctory and expected. He'd made it funny. For a while he counted each hundred-and-eighty-eight strides as an Allen, "a buddy's height in centimeters." While funny at first, he'd given it up when, even with making up numbers, they'd easily crossed several hundred Allens. Then he'd begun counting it out in marathon lengths, but that became even more depressing.

There was a shared closeness to their trudge across the Ionian plains. A shared hardship, but also a shared determination.

She was in point position when they finally reached the "neck," a surface material change rather than an elevation change. She stopped. Parello stumbled up beside her and also inspected the change.

The surface material had been predominantly yellow-gray and brown for the entire day.

Now they stood on the edge of a brighter yellow lava flow, long since solidified. They were on a slight rise that had forced the flow, originating to the south, to narrow here, before spreading wide across the northern plains. The "neck" was narrow enough, barely five kilometers across, that they could see the darker plains beyond. Had they lost their way, they wouldn't be able to see across the width of the flow.

Numb, they stood side by side for a long moment looking down at the goal they'd been chasing for two long days.

"We made it," Parello's voice was soft with disbelief.

All she could do was nod, despite knowing he couldn't see her do so inside her helmet.

Then Parello folded her weary body into his arms and just held her. If she could have kissed him, she would. She fought with hundreds, served with thousands, but this man was the sort she'd always want beside her no matter how sticky the situation.

"Christine the Fighting Machine," his voice little more than a warm caress on her ears.

Together they sunk to their knees and just leaned against each other while their bodies went through the shakes. Pain, so long ignored, pounded up her legs. Muscles cramped, but with nowhere to go and no way to massage them, she just rode it out. Rode it out until at long last they were just holding each other.

Neither spoke before collapsing into exhaustion.

There was no need.

4

The radio crackle inside Christine's helmet was like an alarm clock. She sat bolt upright, dragging herself from the gentle clasp of Parello's suited arms. She'd curse at her stiff and sore muscles later.

"Captain Christine Merrill here." Cursing her slow brain, she swung her chin far right and brought up the tactical display on the inside of her helmet.

A single Stinger ship was cruising toward them, low from the north. Even as she spotted it, it dropped lower and banked in her direction.

Either it was trying to stay below an enemy's radar sweep or—

"Shit!" She silenced her comm, punched the Off switch mounted on Parello's cuff for his comm, then shook him. Shook him hard. Deep sleeper.

She rested her helmet against his and shouted, "Soldier!"

"Huh? What?" He grabbed for his cross-slung rifle, but they were so close, he actually grabbed her chest. Through their visors, she could actually see him blush. It was pretty cute, but she didn't have time for cute.

"Incoming craft," she spoke loudly enough that he'd hear through the helmet-to-helmet conduction.

"Don't think it's one of ours."

"Why?"

"An itch."

He nodded. He clearly knew a soldier stayed alive by trusting that itch.

"Comm on, but handsign only. Roger?"

"Roger, Captain." Then he leaned forward and kissed the inside of his visor. Close as you could come to the real thing in a suit.

What the hell? Be interesting to find out just what it was like to kiss Parello. Really interesting. She returned the gesture, feeling both touched and ridiculous.

She rolled away, restored comm, and, for the first time since the crash, fully powered up her suit. Her heads-up display showed her weapons status; both the pair of launchers built into her pack and the SCAR rifle she'd now pulled free and taken into her hands.

The situational map pinpointed Parello ducking below the rock behind her. From his extra gear he'd grabbed a Demon, a nasty little ground-to-ship handheld missile with a seriously bad-ass attitude. He'd hold that in reserve as a weapon of last resort. If they killed this ship, they might have no way at all off this rock.

She unslung her forty-millimeter rocket tube and tossed it to him. She'd take the meet-and-greet and be ready for forward fire if needed. He'd be the hammer behind, covering her as long as she stayed off to one side.

The Stinger came down, kicking a rolling wall of sulfur that settled quickly enough in the thin atmosphere.

Two troopers dropped to the surface, but rather than approaching, they moved to guard positions on either side of the airlock.

The man who stepped out next made her freeze.

No matter how much training you get, there are some things that you just can't prepare for. She was still frozen, knew she was directly in Parello's line of fire, but she couldn't do a thing about it as the figure strode up to her and stopped just two paces off.

"Hi Chrissy. Haven't seen you in a long, long time."

"Dad."

5

Christine made it clear she wasn't going with
him.

She stood there on the yellow soil and
told the old bastard that she'd rather die
than go with the murderer of her own, loyal
troops.

When he said he'd already killed off the
rescue ship, she informed him of her rank
and serial number, then told "The Sword"
Moore that she'd rather rot on Io than climb
aboard his ship.

She called him a murderer; the worst possible insult to any soldier.

The angrier he grew, the less she cared. Her thoughts drifted to Parello. They were going to die here. Perhaps they were going to die now. It was a pity, a real pity. Before her stood the traitor to the human race, behind her squatted the best man she'd ever known, and there wasn't a chance in hell for them. In Hell. There was the joke. Of the whole solar system, Io was about the closest there was. Fire and brimstone, literally.

Fine.

This is where she and Parello would make their final stand, in Hell.

"No, you are not my father, Generalissimo Traitor Moore. I will fight you until my last breath. I will fight you until this soldier can no longer stand. You will not fly this space without the danger of meeting me as I hunt you down and kill you like a dog."

Peripherally, she was aware of the two guards by the airlock galvanized into action, swinging their rifles up and in her direction.

Her father's eyes widened as four rounds flew close by, two to either side of her helmet—close enough that her visor's audible threat warning system screamed, even though the shots came from behind her.

Parello's rounds punched out the visors of the two guards before they could react.

Even as the guards crumpled, she swung up her SCAR.

Her father did the same.

She was faster to the trigger. She didn't realize that she'd flipped it on full auto until she was emptying the whole load into him.

Still she had the trigger down and the muzzle tracking "The Sword" as he drifted slowly to the ground long after the magazine ran dry.

When Parello came up and gently took the weapon from her hands, she finally came to. Shook her head. Her mind kept trying to think, feel, wonder, be ashamed, be afraid... She shook her head again.

"Tactical?" Some thin thread of her training held her together and asked the key question. It gave her a rope to climb back from where she'd just gone, what she'd just done. Back into the present away from the volcanic anger of the past. Back to the present where she and Parello stood side by side on the Ionian plain of the Shakuru Patera.

"Just the three of them."

"Did I martyr him?" Would the body of "The Sword" become a rallying icon across the system?

"No." Parello sounded so sure. "No, I will make sure it is known far and wide that you defeated him. That his daughter defeated him as he prepared to murder her."

"Known far and wide?"

He stood in front of her, finally breaking her gaze from the lifeless body crumpled before her. The body of a man she no longer knew. Instead, she looked up into those wonderful dark eyes of Parello.

"You can do that?"

"I can." There was no questioning his confidence.

She nodded once, twice, tapped their helmets together for a moment in thanks, then buckled down and did what had to be done. Though she let Parello load "The Sword's" body into the cargo hold on his own. They flew back to the crash site in the captured ship and retrieved the other bodies. Then took off from Hell to spread the word of victory.

The snake wasn't dead yet, but they had certainly cut off its head.

6

"Told you I'd spread the word far and wide."

Christine couldn't argue with that. "Parello" had been true to his word; the length and breadth of the whole system knew who she was and what she'd done. Prince Phillip Allen Richards had indeed been uniquely placed to do so.

The royal heir had served anonymously as so many of England's royalty had done over the centuries. Parello was a play on the "parallels" in his life: serving as his ancestors had, both before and during the Colony Wars, also serving in the Armed forces against the terrorists to defend his own future throne.

Christine was glad that he hadn't told her his true identity until after they'd decided they were totally crazy about each other; a sentiment he also shared and demonstrated delightfully at every opportunity in the two years since the Victory at Io.

And, while she wasn't serving forward military anymore, now that the last of the rebels had finally given up, it was hard to argue with her new title: Major in charge of flying the armored Stinger for the Royal Family.

Including herself and their yet-to-be-born daughter.

They'd already decided to name her Parella after her father.

And when she was grown, and done flying with the Night Stalkers, she would, as her mother now did, wear the infamous Sword of Io.

Once again held by an officer as it should be.

Once again a symbol of honor and country.

About the Author

M. L. Buchman has over 25 novels in print. His military romantic suspense books have been named Barnes & Noble and NPR "Top 5 of the year" and *Booklist* "Top 10 of the Year." In addition to romance, he also writes thrillers, fantasy, and science fiction.

In among his career as a corporate project manager he has: rebuilt and single-handed a fifty-foot sailboat, both flown and jumped out of airplanes, designed and built two houses, and bicycled solo around the world.

He is now making his living full-time as a writer, living on the Oregon Coast with his beloved wife. He is constantly amazed at what you can do with a degree in Geophysics. You may keep up with his writing at www.mlbuchman.com.

Light Up the Night

Second Lieutenant Trisha O'Malley waited ten kilometers off the north coast of Somalia for the mission "Go!" moment. She held her AH-6M Little Bird attack helicopter at wave height, exactly at wave height. The long metal skids were practically being licked clean by the rolling crests heading across the Gulf of Aden.

Through the large openings to either side of the tiny cockpit where the doors would be hung, the smell of the hot night ocean wafted thick with salt and bitter from the dust blown off the achingly dry land. Nobody flew a Little Bird with the doors on. She didn't know why they even ordered them. The only time they were used was to protect the birds when they were parked in harsh enviornments; a piece of plastic could do that. When they flew, the doors were off. Having them off also added freedom of movement to the tiny cockpit and, far more importantly, the visibility was much better.

Not that visibility was such a big deal at the moment. Outside the forward glass-and-polycarbonate windscreen, which reached from below her foot pedals to almost above her head, was nothing but impenetrable darkness. That was one of many things Trisha liked about the Little Birds. The console swept up between the pilots' seats but was confined to a narrow column on the front windscreen that stopped below eye level.

Flying an AH-6M was as close to flying with nothing between you and the sky as existed. No door beside you and bullet-resistant protection from below your feet to farther back than you could tilt your head while wearing a helmet. Everything a girl needed for a good time.

The console itself was dominated by a pair of LCD multifunction screens that could be switched at the tap of a button from engine performance to weather radar to digital terrain map. It made her feel like those science fiction movie heroes in superpowered suits, as if rather than flying a chopper, she herself was wearing a weaponized suit that happened to be in the shape of a helicopter.

Though there really was nothing to see at the moment. Even through her night-vision gear that projected infrared images from the cameras mounted on the outside of the chopper onto the inside of her helmet's visor, there was nothing to see ahead. Except more waves.

To her right hovered the DAP Hawk Vengeance with Chief Warrant 3 Lola Maloney commanding, and beyond that Dusty James's transport Black Hawk, the Vicious. To Trisha's left, if Chief Warrant 2 Roland Emerson weren't sitting shoulder to shoulder with her in his copilot seat, she'd be able to see the two other Little Birds of her flight formation, Mad Max and Merchant of Death—Max and Merchant for short.

When she'd named her bird May, everyone thought it was some stupid woman joke. But any fool who teased her about it being the Merry Month of…or Mayfly soon learned that it was short for Mayhem. She never had to explain it twice.

There was no "Go!" command and no need for risking that extra bit of encrypted communication. The mission "Go" had been given fifteen minutes earlier when they'd spun up their rotors and departed the USS Peleliu amphibious assault ship floating forty miles out in the Arabian Sea.

Now fifteen seconds to start of mission, she wound up on the throttle in her left hand. At five seconds to "Go!" both the bird and Trisha's body were humming with the need to get moving.

The clock on her dash hit 03:00—and she was gone. The May didn't fly, she leaped. Not like a racehorse, like a greyhound. With the collective full up and the cyclic forward, Trisha was tilted nose down five feet above the waves and a hundred meters in the lead of any other bird in the flight, right where she liked to be. They closed formation quickly, but she liked setting a higher standard even on this, her first operational flight. It had been two long years of training and she was way past ready.

Even with the low-noise blades and engine baffles, the roar inside the craft was loud enough that you wouldn't want to try a conversation without your headset. You could do it, but your voice would get tired really fast. Despite the full-enclosure helmet, she could feel the familiar beat of the machine and whine of the high-speed turbine engine against her body.

Everything in tune and running true. Sounded like an idea for a song, not that she could write music.

Three a.m. should be the sleepiest moment on the Somali coast. Intelligence said the guard change was at oh-four-hundred. Everyone else should be asleep.

Everyone except the Night Stalkers of the U.S. Army's 160th Special Operations Aviation Regiment (airborne). SOAR(a) ruled the night, the most elite Special Forces helicopter team on the planet.

Tonight they'd be ruling the northern coastal town of Bosaso, Somalia, on the Horn of Africa. Or at least one corner of it. They wouldn't be engaging within the third largest city in the country, because the pirates had made the mistake of using a compound outside of town. The local authorities were clamping down hard on piracy and, even if just for public image's sake alone, they wouldn't have been as tolerant of the pirates if they were right in town.

She'd expected to feel some serious nerves. It was her first mission-qualified flight for the Night Stalkers. She'd spent five years with the 101st Airborne flying Cobra attack and Little Birds. She had planned that the day she hit the five-year minimum-experience requirement, she'd walk across Fort Campbell and knock on the 160th's locked gate for an application. Instead, an invitation to apply had been waiting for her that very morning.

Trisha smiled even at the memory of that. Her old friend Major Beale had kept track of her despite roaring up the officer ranks. Trisha hadn't West Pointed in, though she could have. Instead she'd made her parents crazy by taking the NYU education that she'd paid for herself, then enlisting and bucking her way up from private. Though stepping back to the basics of Office Candidate School after she'd been a non-commissioned officer for several years had been tough . She didn't want any advantages;she'd long since understood the value of learning the hard way. She'd no more climb up the broad ladder of her father's political heft than she would clamber up the lace-draped tiers of her mother's social one.

Two more years had passed since she'd been accepted to SOAR. She was used to leading entire flights and planning operations for the Screaming Eagles. Not so with the Night Stalkers. They'd spent two years showing her just how little she knew. She was glad to simply be allowed to fly with them.

"One click," Roland said over the headset. She and Roland were the same rank, though he'd been in a year longer than she had. He was there in case she fucked up.

No! Trisha admonished herself. He was there as her copilot. If he were there to cover for her, she'd be in the left seat and he'd be in the right-hand pilot position. All they both cared about was doing this mission and doing it right.

One kilometer out. Fifteen seconds to shore.

Right on cue, the breakwater came into view. A massive pile of car-sized concrete blocks protected the small harbor from storms coming in off the Arabian Sea. But it wasn't ready for the storm that the Night Stalkers could unleash.

# # #

Navy SEAL Lieutenant William Bruce squatted in the dust, wearing the standard clothes of a mercenary soldier looking for a quick buck by joining the Somali pirates. Bill wore camo pants, a dark tank-tee, and a black sweatband. He carried a very battered but immensely serviceable M-16 which marked him even more clearly as a merc for bringing his own weapon with him.

Most pirates wielded out-of-date Russian crap, some of it from all the way back to WWII, that was as likely to explode in their hands as to actually fire. He had a Russian TT-30 semi-auto pistol in the back of his waistband, a reliable enough weapon though he preferred a Sig Sauer, spare magazines in his thigh pouches, and a rusting but very sharp hunting knife strapped to his thigh. He fit right in.

Bill checked his watch. Oh-three-hundred sharp.

The choppers should be here in three minutes, if they were to be trusted. There was a laugh. A decade in the Navy, the last five years as a SEAL, and he still didn't trust the Night Stalkers. He really should try to get over it, but he didn't see that happening anytime soon. They were dead reliable, anywhere on the planet, any time. But this was Somalia, and though it wasn't their fault, he couldn't help himself. He would never trust them on Somali soil.

Available at fine retailers everywhere
Sept, 2014

More information at:
www.mlbuchman.com

Other works by M.L. Buchman

The Night Stalkers
The Night Is Mine
I Own the Dawn
Daniel's Christmas
Wait Until Dark
Frank's Independence Day
Peter's Christmas
Take Over at Midnight
Light Up the Night

Firehawks
Pure Heat
Wildfire at Dawn
Full Blaze

Angelo's Hearth
Where Dreams are Born
Where Dreams Reside
Maria's Christmas Table
Where Dreams Unfold
Where Dreams Are Written

Dieties Anonymous
Cookbook from Hell: Reheated
Saviors 101

Thrillers
Swap Out!
One Chef

SF/F Titles
Nara

Monk's Maze